What About HARRY?

by Derek Anderson

HARPER
An Imprint of HarperCollinsPublishers

For information address HarperCollins
Children's Books, a division of HarperCollins
Publishers, 195 Broadway, New York, NY 10007.
www.harpercollinschildrens.com

ISBN 978-0-06-240259-2

The artist used ink and Photoshop to
create the illustrations for this book.
Typography by Rachel Zegar
18 19 20 21 22 SCP 10 9 8 7 6 5 4 3 2 1
❖
First Edition

For Derek, Rachel,
Riley, and Audrey Nash

Sam and Harry are best friends.
They do everything together.
"What do you want to play today?" asks Harry.

"Let's be kings!" says Sam.
"First we need crowns."

"My crown is going to be fancy," says Harry.

"What do kings do?" asks Harry.
"Kings live in castles," says Sam.
"We can build them right here."

"My castle is going to
be BIG," says Harry.

"We are kings of everything," says Sam. "Even the swings."

"I'm going to swing the highest," says Harry.

Look at how high Sam is!

"Every king needs a royal portrait. Let's paint our own," says Sam.

"Come on, Harry," yells Sam.
"Let's be kings of the pond."

"YOU THINK SAM IS SO GREAT?
WATCH THIS!"

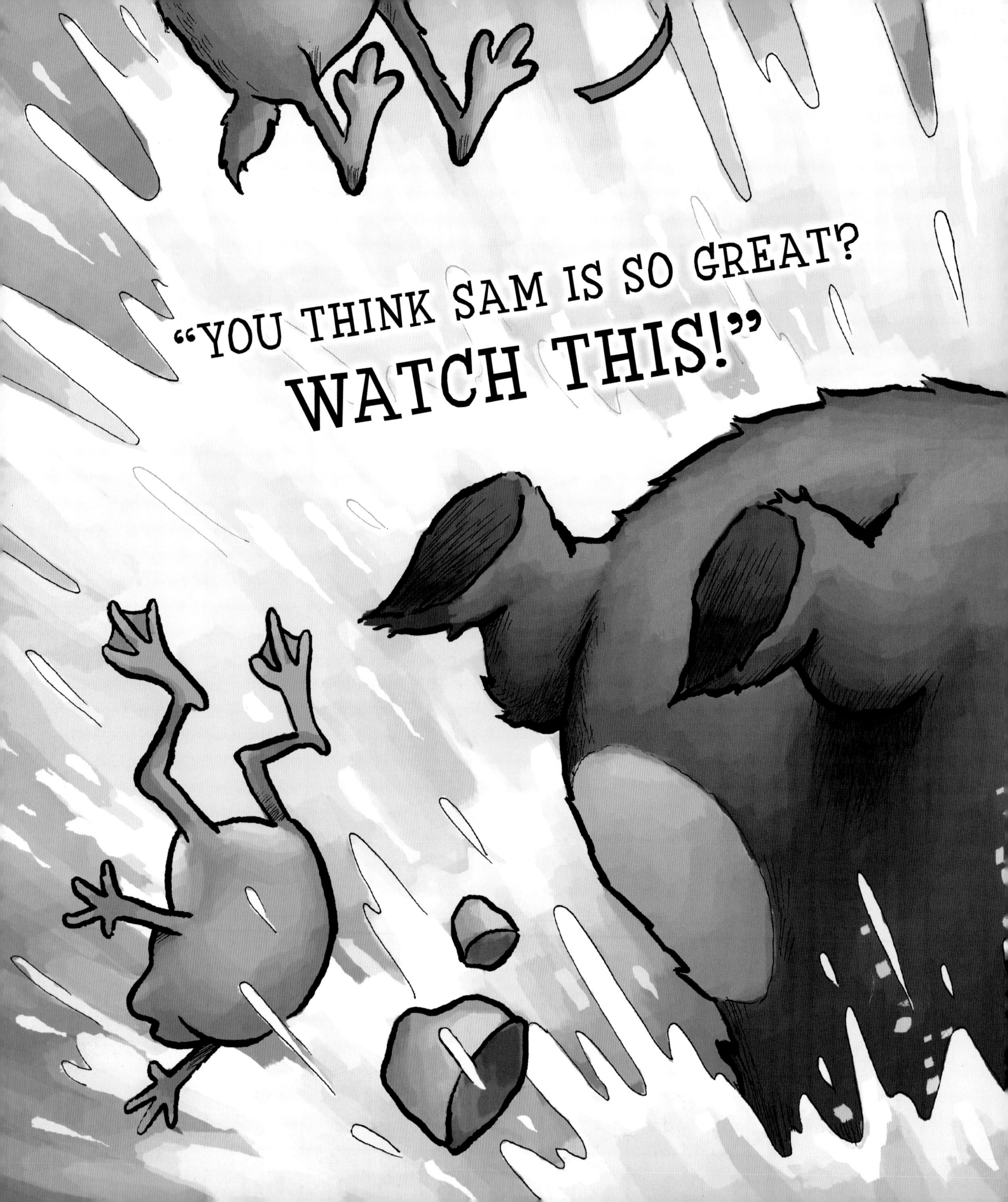

"Harry?" says Sam.

"I'm going to be king all by myself," growls Harry.

Harry builds a new castle.

He's king of a new swing.

He makes his own royal yacht.

But it isn't the same without Sam.

Sam misses Harry.

Harry misses Sam.

Suddenly, Harry gets an idea!

"Sam, Sam, I have to tell you something," cries Harry. "I'm sorry I splashed you." "That's okay," says Sam. "What's that?"

"I made a picture for you,"
says Harry.
"That's the best picture in
the world!" says Sam.

"What happened to your crown?" asks Sam.

"I don't have it anymore," says Harry.

"Here, take mine," says Sam.

"Come on, you have to show me how to make a splash like you did before."

"You are the KING of splashes!"